Author's Note

The practice of yoga naturally lends itself to children because many yoga poses imitate things we find in nature. Children love to pretend they are trees or animals, and as they imitate the natural world around them, they connect with it and appreciate it on a deeper level.

Yoga is normally practiced barefoot for better balance and grip. (A sticky mat is useful but not essential.) Yoga is not about competition. Listen to your body. Never push yourself or force the postures. Keep your body relaxed and your breath slow and steady.

Namaste (Na-mah-stay). (The spirit in me honors the spirit in you.)

—Kathy Beliveau

For my husband, Tim, who sees the world in a grain of sand and a forest in a tiny seed. Thank you for our endless, enchanting gardens. -K.B.

For Courtney, you had me at Courtney. -D.H.

Published in 2016 by Simply Read Books www.simplyreadbooks.com

Text © 2016 Kathy Beliveau
Illustrations © 2016 Denise Holmes

Library and Archives Canada Cataloguing in Publication
Beliveau, Kathy, 1962-, author
The yoga game in the garden / written by Kathy
Beliveau ; illustrated by Denise Holmes.

ISBN 978-1-927018-71-2 (bound)
1. Hatha yoga--Juvenile literature. I. Holmes, Denise,
illustrator II. Title.

RA781.7.B454 2015   j613.7'046   C2014-906178-1

We gratefully acknowledge for their financial support of our publishing program the Canada Council for the Arts, the BC Arts Council, and the Government of Canada through the Canada Book Fund (CBF).

Manufactured in Korea.

Book design by Sara Gillingham Studio.

10 9 8 7 6 5 4 3 2 1

THE YOGA GAME

IN THE GARDEN

by Kathy Beliveau • illustrated by Denise Holmes

SIMPLY READ BOOKS

Wiggle your toes and touch your nose.
Now can you guess the yoga pose?
First we listen to the clue,
then we see what we can do!

Softer than a breath, that's me.
I'm known to be bumbly.
A ball of black and yellow fuzz;
my song is like a low, deep buzzzz.

What am I?

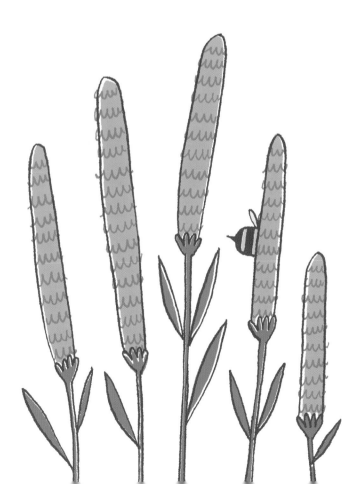

hummmmmm

I am a **bumblebee!**

I am fuzzy, long and small.
Munching leaves is best of all!
I am a hungry little guy.
I turn into a butterfly.

What am I?

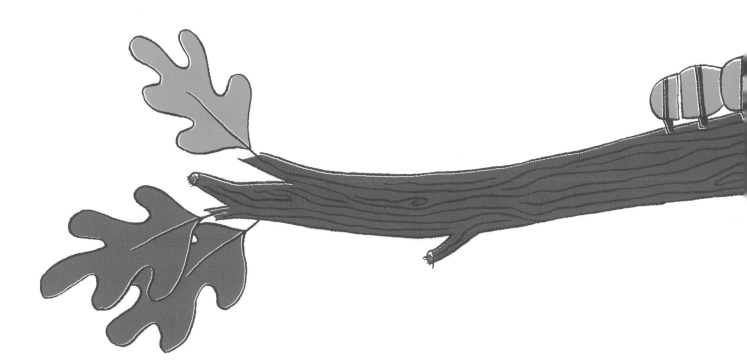

I am a **caterpillar!**

I flit and flutter everywhere,
happy, free, as light as air.
With silent grace, I land on things,
and sunlight dances on my wings.

What am I?

I love a place that's warm and nice
to rest my paws and dream of mice,
where in between my nap and snack,
there's time to arch and stretch my back.

What am I?

I am a **cat!**

I'm known to be man's best friend,
faithful to the very end.
I run, I jump, I bark, I fetch,
and then I pause my paws to stretch.

What am I?

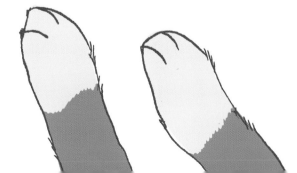

I am a **dog!**

Firmly planted in the ground,
I stand tall and send roots down.
Limbs and branches growing high,
reaching up to touch the sky.

What am I?

The squishy mud of lakes and ponds
inspires me to sing my songs.
I croak, I swim, I hop about.
I squat and stick my tongue way out.

What am I?

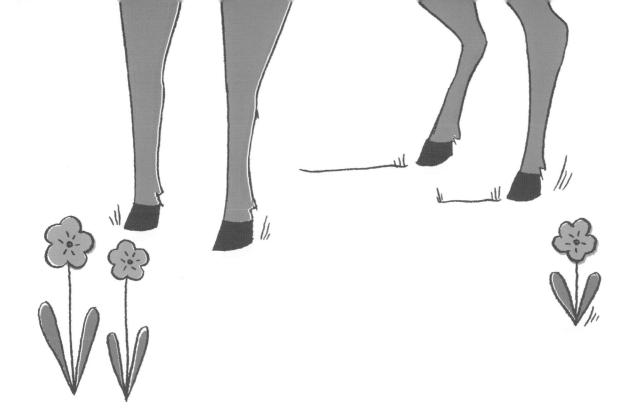

A warm, brown coat, a steady gaze.
I move slowly as I graze.
I might have antlers on my head.
My hoofprints mark the garden bed.

What am I?

I twitch my nose. I nibble and crunch.
I love sweet carrots for my lunch.
I have long ears and hop around,
but almost never make a sound.

What am I?

My petals are a pretty sight,
blooms and blossoms of delight.
Gather me for a bouquet,
to celebrate a special day.

What am I?

I am a **flower!**

I breathe the air, the air breathes me.
I am the land. I am the sea.
I am the clouds that drift above.
I am special. I am love.

What am I?

I am **me!**

Namaste.